1918466

PowerKids Readers:

The Bilingual Library of the United States of America™

Bilingual Edition
English / Spanish
Edición bilingüe

MISSISSIPPI

MISISIPI

VANESSA BROWN

TRADUCCIÓN AL ESPAÑOL: MARÍA CRISTINA BRUSCA

The Rosen Publishing Group's
PowerKids Press™ & **Editorial Buenas Letras**™
New York

Published in 2006 by The Rosen Publishing Group, Inc.
29 East 21st Street, New York, NY 10010

First Edition

Book Design: Albert B. Hanner
Photo Credits: Cover, pp. 9, 21, 31 (plantation) © Buddy Mays/Corbis; pp. 5, 30 (state motto) © Joseph Sohm; Chromosohm Inc./Corbis; pp. 7, 31 (border) © 2002 Geoaltlas; p. 11, 30 (Magnolia Tree) © Patrick Johns/Corbis; p. 13 The New York Public Library/Art Resource, NY; pp. 15, 17, 31 (Faulkner, Hamer, Presley) © Bettmann/Corbis; p. 19 Library of Congress Prints and Photographs Division; pp. 23, 31 (rural) © Danny Lehman/Corbis; pp. 25, 30 (capital) © Philip Gould/Corbis; pp. 26, 30 (state flower, state nickname) © Peter Smithers/Corbis; p. 30 (Mockingbird) © Joe McDonald/Corbis; p. 30 (Mozarkite) Albert Hanner; p. 31 (explorer) © PoodlesRock/Corbis; p. 31 (King) © Neal Preston/Corbis; p. 31 (Winfrey) © Steve Sands/New York Newswire/Corbis, p. 31 (Rice) © Reuters/Corbis

Library of Congress Cataloging-in-Publication Data

Brown, Vanessa, 1963–
Mississippi / Vanessa Brown ; traducción al español, María Cristina Brusca.— 1st ed.
p. cm. — (The bilingual library of the United States of America) Includes bibliographical references and index.
ISBN 1-4042-3089-0 (library binding)
1. Mississippi–Juvenile literature. I. Title. II. Series.
F466.3.B76 2006
976.2—dc22
                                                                    2005010833

Manufactured in the United States of America

Due to the changing nature of Internet links, Editorial Buenas Letras has developed an online list of Web sites related to the subject of this book. This site is updated regularly. Please use this link to access the list:

http://www.buenasletraslinks.com/ls/mississippi

Contents

Contenido

Welcome to Mississippi

These are the flag and seal of the state of Mississippi. A bald eagle is in the center of the seal. The bald eagle is the national bird of the United States.

Bienvenidos a Misisipi

Estos son la bandera y el escudo del estado de Misisipi. En el centro del escudo hay un águila calva. El águila calva es el ave nacional de los Estados Unidos.

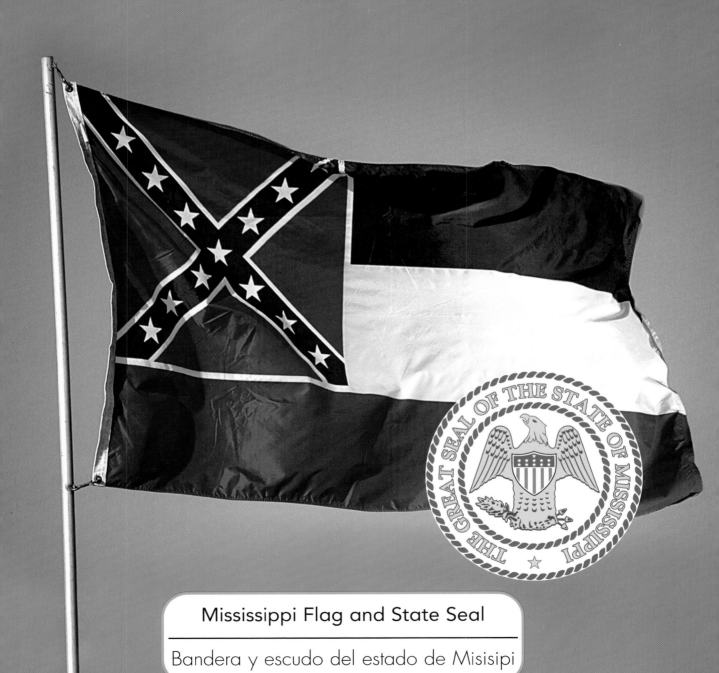

Mississippi Flag and State Seal

Bandera y escudo del estado de Misisipi

Mississippi Geography

Mississippi borders the states of Tennessee, Alabama, Louisiana, and Arkansas. On the south, Mississippi borders the Gulf of Mexico.

Geografía de Misisipi

Misisipi linda con los estados de Tennessee, Alabama, Luisiana y Arkansas. En el sur, Misisipi linda con el golfo de México.

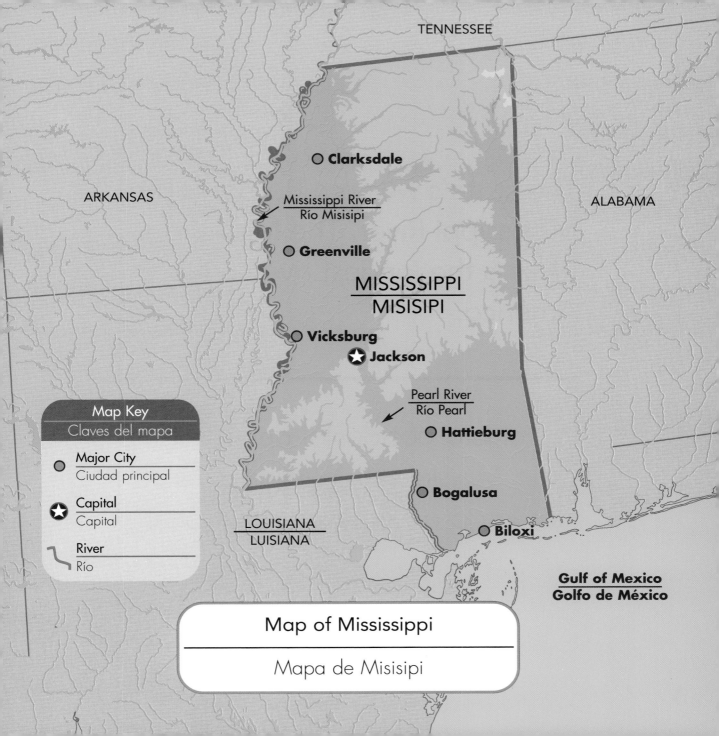

TENNESSEE

ARKANSAS

ALABAMA

◎ **Clarksdale**

Mississippi River
Río Misisipi

◎ **Greenville**

MISSISSIPPI
MISISIPI

◉ **Vicksburg**

⭐ **Jackson**

Pearl River
Río Pearl

◎ **Hattieburg**

LOUISIANA
LUISIANA

◎ **Bogalusa**

◎ **Biloxi**

Gulf of Mexico
Golfo de México

Map Key
Claves del mapa

◉ Major City
Ciudad principal

⭐ Capital
Capital

〰 River
Río

Map of Mississippi

Mapa de Misisipi

The state's western border is the Mississippi River. The Mississippi River is the longest river in North America.

La frontera occidental del estado es el río Misisipi. El río Misisipi es el más largo de América del Norte.

Delta Queen Riverboat on the Mississippi River

Barco *Delta Queen* en el río Missisipi

Mississipi is known as the Magnolia State. The magnolia is both Mississippi's state flower and state tree.

Misisipi es conocido como el Estado de la Magnolia. La magnolia es la flor del estado y también es el árbol del estado.

A Flowering Magnolia

Una magnolia florecida

Mississippi History

Five hundred years ago three Native American groups lived in Mississippi. The Natchez lived in the southwest, the Chickasaw lived in the north, the Choctaw lived in the south-central area of the state.

Historia de Misisipi

Hace quinientos años, vivían en Misisipi tres grupos indígenas americanos. Los Natchez vivían en el sudoeste, los Chickasaw vivían en el norte y los Choctaw vivían en el área centro-sur del estado.

Native Americans with European Explorers

Nativos americanos con exploradores europeos

In 1540, Hernando de Soto became the first European to reach Mississippi. De Soto was a Spanish explorer. He died in 1542. His body was dropped from a boat into the Mississippi River.

En 1540, Hernando de Soto se convirtió en el primer europeo en llegar a Misisipi. De Soto fue un explorador español. Murió en 1542. Su cuerpo fue echado desde un bote al río Misisipi.

Hernando de Soto

Cotton was the main crop in Mississippi in the 1800s. Owners of big farms called plantations used African slaves to collect cotton. Slaves were people owned by the plantation owners.

En los años 1800, el algodón era el principal cultivo de Misisipi. Los dueños de las grandes granjas, llamadas plantaciones, usaban esclavos africanos para cosechar el algodón. Los esclavos eran propiedad de los dueños de las plantaciones.

Slaves Picking Cotton in Field

Esclavos cosechando algodón en el campo

The use of slaves was one cause of the Civil War. The Civil War was fought between the Northern states and the Southern states from 1861 to 1865. The Battle of Vicksburg was an important battle fought in Mississippi.

El uso de esclavos fue una de las causas de la Guerra Civil. La Guerra Civil fue una guerra entre los estados del Norte y los estados del Sur de 1861 a 1865. La Batalla de Vicksburg fue una batalla muy importante en Misisipi.

The Battle of Vicksburg

La Batalla de Vicksburg

Living in Mississippi

Natchez, Mississippi, is one of the oldest cities in the United States. Many big homes that were built in the 1800s still have their original beauty.

La vida en Misisipi

Natchez, Misisipi, es una de las ciudades más antiguas de los Estados Unidos. Muchas grandes casas, que fueron construídas en los años 1800, todavía mantienen su belleza original.

The Stanton Hall Mansion Was Built in 1858

La mansión Stanton Hall, construida en 1858

Mississippi has one of the largest rural populations in the United States. This means that many Mississippians live on farms or in small towns in the countryside.

Misisipi tiene una de las poblaciones rurales más grandes de los Estados Unidos. Esto quiere decir que muchos misisipianos viven en granjas o en pequeños pueblos de campo.

The Town of Clarksdale, Mississippi

El pueblo de Clarksdale, Misisipi

Jackson, Gulfport, Biloxi, and Hattiesburg are important cities in Mississippi. Jackson is the most-populated city and the capital of the state.

Jackson, Gulfport, Biloxi y Hattiesburg son ciudades importantes de Misisipi, Jackson es la ciudad más poblada del estado. Jackson es la capital de Misisipi.

The Mississippi State Capitol in Jackson

Capitolio del estado de Misisipi, en Jackson

Activity:
Let's Draw Mississippi's State Flower

The magnolia became Mississippi's state flower in 1952.

Actividad:
Dibujemos la flor del estado de Misisipi

La magnolia es la flor del estado de Misisipi desde 1952

1

Draw the center circle. Then draw four circles around the center.

Dibuja el círculo central. Luego dibuja cuatro círculos alrededor del centro.

Add slightly larger half circles around the first four circles.

2

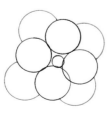

Agrega algunos medio círculos, un poco más grandes, alrededor de los cinco primeros círculos.

3

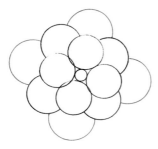

Draw four more half circles as shown.

Dibuja otros cuatro medio círculos, como en la muestra.

4

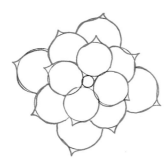

Use the circles and half circles to shape the petals. Be sure to draw the pointed tips.

Usa los círculos y los medio círculos para dar forma a los pétalos. Asegúrate de dibujar las puntas agudas.

5

Erase extra lines. Add shading and lines to your magnolia.

Borra las líneas innecesarias. Agrega líneas y sombras a tu magnolia.

Timeline		Cronología
Hernando de Soto becomes the first European to explore Mississippi.	**1540**	Hernando de Soto es el primer europeo en explorar Misisipi.
Mississippi becomes part of Louisiana, under French control.	**1682**	Misisipi forma parte de Luisiana y pertenece a Francia.
U.S. Congress creates the Mississippi Territory.	**1789**	El congreso de los Estados Unidos crea el Territorio de Misisipi.
Mississippi becomes the twentieth state of the Union.	**1817**	Misisipi pasa a ser el vigésimo estado de la Unión.
Mississippi leaves the Union and becomes a Confederate state.	**1861**	Misisipi abandona la Unión y se convierte en un estado de la Confederación.
Mississippi is readmitted to the Union.	**1870**	Misisipi es readmitido en la Unión.
James Meredith becomes the first African American to attend the University of Mississippi.	**1962**	James Meredith es el primer afroamericano en asistir a la Universidad de Misisipi.

Mississippi Events

April
Natchez Trace Festival in Kosciusko
World Catfish Festival
in Humphreys County

May
Atwood Bluegrass Festival
in Monticello
Civil War Reenactment in Vicksburg

July
Choctaw Indian Fair in Philadephia
Watermelon Festival in Mize

September
Mississippi Delta Blues and Heritage
Festival in Greenville
Seafood Festival in Biloxi

October
Mississippi State Fair in Jackson

December
Christmas in Natchez
Trees of Christmas Festival in
Meridian

Eventos en Misisipi

Abril
Festival de la Ruta Natchez, en Kosciusko
Festival mundial del barbo, en el condado
de Humpreys

Mayo
Festival de bluegrass Atwood, en
Monticello
Representación de la Guerra Civil, en
Vicksburg

Julio
Feria de la Tribu Choctaw, en Filadelfia
Festival de la sandía, en Mize

Septiembre
Festival de la tradición y el blues del
Delta del Misisipi, en Greenville
Festival de los pescados y mariscos, en
Biloxi

Octubre
Feria del estado de Misisipi, en Jackson

Diciembre
Navidad en Natchez
Festival de los árboles de Navidad, en
Meridian

Mississippi Facts/Datos sobre Misisipi

Population
2.8 million

Población
2.8 millones

Capital
Jackson

Capital
Jackson

State Motto
By Valor and Arms

Lema del estado
Por el valor y por las armas

State Flower
Magnolia

Flor del estado
Magnolia

State Bird
Mockingbird

Ave del estado
Sinsonte

State Nickname
The Magnolia State

Mote del estado
El Estado de las Magnolias

State Tree
Magnolia tree

Árbol del estado
Magnolia

State Song
"Go Mississippi"

Canción del estado
"Adelante Misisipi"

State Gemstone
Mozarkite
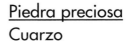
Piedra preciosa
Cuarzo

Famous Mississippians/Misisipianos famosos

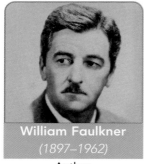

William Faulkner
(1897–1962)

Author
Escritor

Fannie Lou Hamer
(1917–1977)

Activist
Activista

B. B. King
(1925—   )

Blues guitarist and singer
Guitarrista y cantante de blues

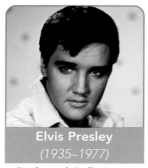

Elvis Presley
(1935–1977)

Rock–and–Roll singer
Cantante de rock and roll

Oprah Winfrey
(1954–   )

Television entertainer
Animadora de televisión

Jerry Rice
(1962–   )

Football player
Jugador de fútbol americano

Words to Know/Palabras que debes saber

border
frontera

explorer
explorador

plantation
plantación

rural
rural

31

Here are more books to read about Mississippi:
Otros libros que puedes leer sobre Misisipi:

In English/En inglés:

Mississippi: The Magnolia State
World Almanac Library of the States
by Figueroa, Acton
World Almanac Library, 2003

Mississippi
America the Beautiful
by George, Charles and George, Linda
Children's Press, 1999

Words in English: 297

Palabras en español: 323

Index

Índice